DrRoach

First published in Great Britain in 2012 by Boxer Books Limited.

www.boxerbooks.com

Based on an original idea by Sam Williams.

Monstrous Stories™ concept, names, stories, designs and logos
© Boxer Books Limited

Written by Paul Harrison
Paul Harrison asserts his moral right to be identified
as the author of this work.
Text copyright © 2012 Boxer Books Limited

Illustrated by Tom Knight
Tom Knight asserts his moral right to be identified
as the illustrator of this work.
Illustrations copyright © 2012 Tom Knight

The illustrations were prepared using brush, ink and digital.
The text is set in Blackmoor Plain and Adobe Caslon.

ISBN 978-1-907967-36-8

1 3 5 7 9 10 8 6 4 2

Printed and bound by CPI Group (UK) Ltd, Croydon, CR0 4YY

All of our papers are sourced from managed forests and renewable resources.

Dr Roach's Monstrous STORIES

Dr Roach presents

THE DAY THE MICE STOOD STILL

a Boxer Books production

Contents

Dr Roach welcomes YOU!

Have you ever seen a flying saucer?

What can make all the mice in a small town suddenly stand still? A giant cheese? A huge mousetrap?

No - a flying saucer from outer space! Alien cats have come to Earth in search of an endless supply of fresh milk. They are shrinking all the cows and are ready to fly off with them.

Will the alien cats pull off their purr-fect plan?
Will the cows be making mini-moos?
Will someone stop them?
Jilly McCafferty will-because she also has a plan.

How, you ask? Come closer, my friend, and I'll tell you all about it.

Welcome to Dr Roach's Monstrous Stories.
Enjoy!

Dr Roach

"Eeeeeeeeekkkkkkkk!"

Jilly McCafferty sat bolt upright in bed. Was that a scream?

"Eeeeeeeeekkkkkkk!"

Yep, that was a scream alright, and it came from the kitchen. Jilly leapt out of bed like a scalded cat and raced into the room. Her mother was

there, perched on a chair, her knees
knocking so hard with fear that the
chair was rattling across the floor like
a crab in a mad hurry.

"Mum, what's wrong?" she asked.

"M-m-m-m-mouse," she
stammered, pointing to the corner of
the room.

"Oh Mum, get a grip, we live on a farm! You should be used to mice by now!" said Jilly, walking over to where the mouse was. "Look, it's friendly; it's not even running away."

9

The mouse was standing perfectly still. Jilly got closer and closer and still the mouse stood there. Jilly went right up to it and touched it.

"I think it's dead," she said. "No, it's still breathing, but it's like it's frozen stiff. Weird."

Mrs McCafferty got down from her chair and nervously edged over.

"Well, it's still horrible – put it outside, and then you'd better get ready for school."

Jilly scooped up the mouse – but she had no intention of just leaving it outside. Nothing exciting ever

happened in Buffalo Bottom, the town where Jilly lived. It was tiny and mostly made up of small farms. This was the best thing to have happened in ages.

"You, my furry friend, are coming to school," she whispered, as she slipped the rigid rodent into her school bag.

The doors to the school bus were barely open before Jilly had leapt on. She quickly found her best friend, Rod, and plopped down on the seat next to him.

"Rod – you're not going to believe this!" said Jilly. Proudly, she lifted the mouse out of her bag.

13

"I bet you've never seen anything like this bef…" her words faded away. Rod was holding a stiffened mouse exactly like hers.

"And we're not the only ones," said Rod. "Show her, everyone."

All over the bus, the school kids held up boxes and bags with frozen mice in them. Everywhere Jilly

looked there were mice: on the luggage racks, in the pockets of the seats – even one on the dashboard of the bus.

"There were mice everywhere," Jilly told her mum that evening.

"Ooh, I know, I've never seen so many – I've been finding them around the farm all day. Disgusting!"

Mrs McCafferty replied. "Anyway, young missy, it's time for bed."

Reluctantly, Jilly made her way upstairs. It took her ages to get to sleep. This mice thing was just too weird. Eventually, she tried counting them – they worked as well as sheep – and soon she was fast asleep.

Eeeeeeeeeeeeeeeyyyyyyyyyyyy
oooooowwwwwwwww!

Jilly woke up with a start and sat
bolt upright! The house was filled
with bright light. What on earth was
that? There was something in the
yard.

"Mum!"

Chapter 3
Flying Saucer

Jilly rushed out of her room and ran straight into her mum.

"What's happening?" asked her mum.

"There's only one way to find out," said Jilly. "Come on."

Jilly grabbed her mother's hand and dragged her out of the house.

"I'm not sure this is a good idea," her mum protested. "It could be anything out there… we're not expecting visitors."

But, expected or not, visitors they had. A large, silver, saucer-shaped spaceship had landed in the farmyard.

Lights flashed around the middle of the craft, and small clouds of steam burst from flaps here and there.

"It's, it's, it's…" Mrs McCafferty stammered.

"A spaceship!" said Jilly.

"I'm calling the police!" said Mrs McCafferty, dashing into the house.

"I'm calling Rod!" said Jilly, dashing for her mobile.

* * *

Within the hour, Jilly's farm was filled with curious people from Buffalo Bottom all watching the spaceship and waiting for something to happen.

HHHIIIIIIIISSSSSSSSSSSS!

A door opened, and a ramp was lowered to the ground.

 The light from
inside the
spaceship was
so bright it was
impossible to
see properly.

The outline of a tall figure appeared
and began to descend the steps. It
seemed to be wearing a cape and had
what looked like two points on the
top of its head.

"Is it the two pointy-headed
monster from Jupiter?" cried one of
the townsfolk.

"Is it the alien
vampire from
Mars?"
shouted
another.

The figure moved out of the
blinding light, and the crowd saw it
properly.

"No, it's a cat!" said Jilly.

Chapter 4
Alien Furr Ball

The cat was taller than the tallest human, walking on its hind legs and wearing a silver cape. It held up a paw to silence the crowd.

"Heuwww! Heuwwwwww!" said
the cat alien.

"Errr, sorry?" said Rod.

"Maybe it can't breathe our air and
it's choking," said Mrs McCafferty.

"Heuwww! Heuwww! Ptah!" The
alien cat spat out a large hairball.

"Euuuurrrgggh!" said the crowd.

"Sorry about that," the cat replied in a silky voice. "My name is Felix Andromedus. I come from the planet Felinus–my crew and I come in peace. Take me to your milk… I mean, take me to your leader."

The mayor was pushed to the front of the crowd.

"Leader of the Earth people," began the cat.

"I don't lead all the people of Earth," the mayor said.

"Ah, of course, you must be the president of the U.S.A. then," the cat replied.

"Mayor," the mayor explained, "of Buffalo Bottom."

The cat looked like it was struggling to understand.

"Very well, President Mayor's Bottom, we have been monitoring your planet, and we have detected your mouse problem.

We have a proposal for you. We shall rid you of these mice in return for... milk!"

"Well, that seems like an excellent idea. On behalf of the good people of Buffalo Bottom, I accept," said the mayor.

Chapter 5
Lost Cows

The next few days were very
exciting. No one ever visited Buffalo
Bottom, but now there were giant
cat aliens all over town. Apart from
the occasional hairball, they were
good to have around, and – being
cats – they were very tidy. Plus, the

mice were gone. But that wasn't the only thing going missing. There were problems at the McCafferty farm, and Jilly was worried.

"What's wrong?" Rod asked Jilly on the way to school.

"We've lost some cows," said Jilly.

"Cows are huge – how can you

lose one of them?"
asked Rod.

"I reckon those
cats have got
something to do
with it," Jilly replied. "Something
isn't right,
and it only started when they
arrived in town."

"People always blame strangers when things go wrong," said Rod. "I mean, where would the aliens keep cows?"

Jilly didn't know, but as sure as cats like milk, she was going to find out.

* * *

That night, Jilly hid herself in the cow barn and waited. She was just beginning to fall asleep when she heard noises.

"Cats!" whispered Jilly to herself. "What are they up to?"

"This is too easy!" laughed one of the cats.

"Humans – they will believe any rubbish! Even the mice knew we were coming – frozen stiff out of fear! And rightly so!" said the other cat.

He pointed a ray gun at a cow.

BAZAM!

A beam of light shot out, the cow glowed and then shrunk to the size of a mouse.

"Once we're home on Felinus, a simple blast of the gun and the cows are back to full size; and we'll have all the milk we want!"

"And we leave tonight, so we need to shrink them all."

And they laughed their terrible alien cat laugh:

"Meow-how-how, meow-how-how, meow-how-how!"

Chapter 6
Ray Guns

The cats shrank the rest of the cows and carried them off to the spaceship.

"I've got to get in there and rescue those cows!" said Jilly.

There was no one on the ramp into the spaceship, so Jilly took her chance and sprinted over to it. A quick peek up the ramp — all clear.

"Well, it's now or never," muttered Jilly, and she crept inside as quickly as she could. The ship was bright, shiny and very, very clean. Jilly slipped down the corridor and turned a corner – a cat! She ducked into a room before she was spotted and silently shut the door.

"Moo."

Jilly span round; she was in a large room piled high with crates of milk – and full of tiny cows!

"Result!" whispered Jilly. "Now, what was it they said? Something about using the gun again... I wonder if it's one of these?"

Jilly took a ray gun off the wall.

Then she emptied a crate of milk cartons and filled it with cows instead.

"And what do you think you're doing?"

Felix, the leader of the cats, stood in the doorway, with the rest of his crew behind him.

"Getting out of here!" said Jilly.
She pointed the ray gun at the cows.
"Stop her!" shouted Felix.

Too late.

MAZAB!

A blast of light
covered the cows.
The box shook,
bulged, then
ripped apart
as the cows got
bigger and bigger.

"Come on,
girls!" shouted Jilly.
"We're going home!"

Chapter 7
The Chase

The cows charged out of the room with Jilly close behind them. The cats were scattered this way and that.

Down the corridor went the herd and down the ramp to freedom!

"What's all the noise?" asked Mrs McCafferty, dashing into the yard.

"It's the aliens, Mum! They're trying to steal the cows – get help!"

The cats, battered and bruised, rose unsteadily to their feet.

"She's taken our cows!" said one.

"Worse than that," said Felix, "look at the state of our spaceship!"

It was covered in cow poo.

* * *

Word spread quickly around Buffalo Bottom. Soon, a crowd had gathered at the farm, just as the spaceship took off.

Eeeeeeeeeeeeeeyyyyyyyyyyyyy ooooooowwwwwwww!

It hovered above the McCafferty farm.

"President Mayor's Bottom, people of Earth, you have displeased us!" came Felix's voice over the loudspeaker. "Prepare to be destroyed … as soon as we have tidied up in here. We shall be back!"

With that, the spaceship zoomed into space.

"Listen, everyone," shouted Jilly.

"They might be super-advanced aliens, but they're still just cats. And we're not going to get beaten by a load of moggies!"

"But what are we going to do?" bleated the mayor.

"I've got a plan," Jilly replied. "Rod, we're going to need all the sheep from your farm – and everyone else's farm, too. And Mum, get the crop-dusting plane ready for take-off. We're going to show these kitties who's boss!"

Chapter 8
Great Balls of Wool

The good people of Buffalo Bottom worked through the night. They sheared the sheep and spun the wool. By daybreak they had a ball of wool the size of a house. And just in time...

51

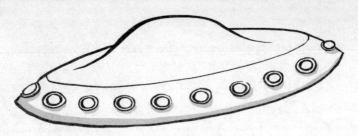

Eeeeeeeeeeeeeeeyyyyyyyyyyyy
oooooowwwwwwwww!

"Puny Earthlings," boomed
Felix's voice, "prepare to meet your
do… hold on a moment, what's that?
Oooohhhh, wool!"

"Got them!" said Jilly to Rod.
"Right, tie the end to Mum's plane."

"Earthlings! Give us the wool and we might spare your worthless lives!"

"Come and get it, furball!" said Jilly. She jumped into the passenger seat of her mother's crop-dusting plane. It was only an old-fashioned bi-plane, but Mrs McCafferty was the best pilot in the state. The engine spluttered into life, and they were off, dragging the wool ball into the air behind them.

"After them!" cried Felix.

"OK, Mum," shouted Jilly over the noise of the engine, "you fly, I'll direct. Take a right into the canyon."

Zoooooom went the plane. Eeeeeeyyyyyyyyyooooowwwwwww went the spaceship, as it followed the plane around the rocky cliff faces of the canyon.

Now left!" said Jilly.

Zooooooom

Eeeeeeeyyyyyyyyyyoooowwwwww.

"Now right!"

Zoooooooom.

Eeeeeeeyyyyyyyyyyoooowwwwww.

The spaceship was almost

upon them.

"Pull up, NOW!"
The nippy little bi-plane suddenly

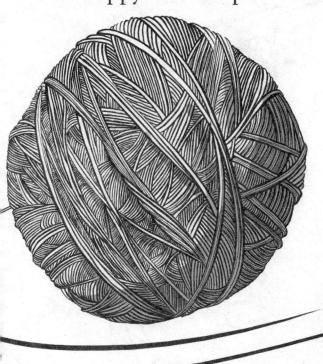

shot straight up the side of the
canyon.

Zooooooom.

But the spaceship didn't!

Eeeeeeeyyyyyyyyyy**CCCCRRRR
AAAASSSSSHHHHHH!**

The battered spaceship lay in
a crumpled heap on the ground.
Then, with a cough, it finally rose
up, rattling back up into the sky and
tearing off into outer space.

The bi-plane landed beside the
cheering townsfolk.

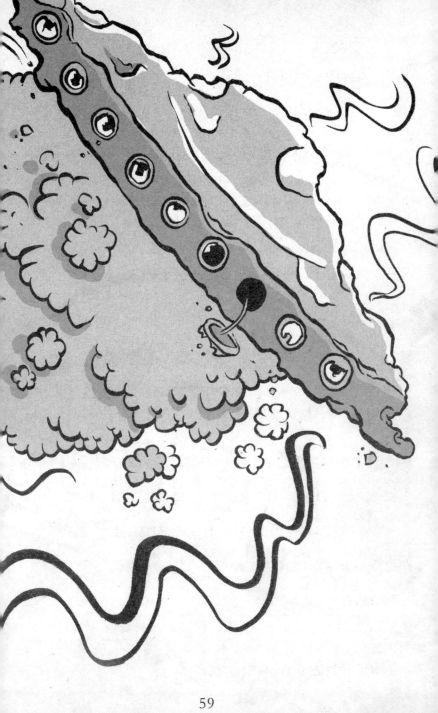

"I reckon that's the last we'll see of them," said Jilly.

"In a way, it's a shame they're gone; it was nice having visitors," said the mayor.

"And we'll have visitors again," said Rod, "now that Jilly's

Welcome to BUFFALO BOTTOM

HOME OF THE WORLD'S LARGEST BALL OF WOOL

given us our new
tourist attraction
– the world's
largest ball
of wool!"

Dr Roach's Monstrous STORIES

FROGOSAURUS VS. THE BOG MONSTER

Do you have a favourite place? Sammy and Tammy do. They love the quiet boggy marshes full of insects and strange plants.

Meet Maximus Sneer. An evil man with lots of money and a secret plan. He is going to drain the boggy marshes dry and then build houses and shops and car parks.

But instead of creating homes he makes two giant monsters-without even knowing it.

How, you ask? Get a copy today, and I'll tell you everything!

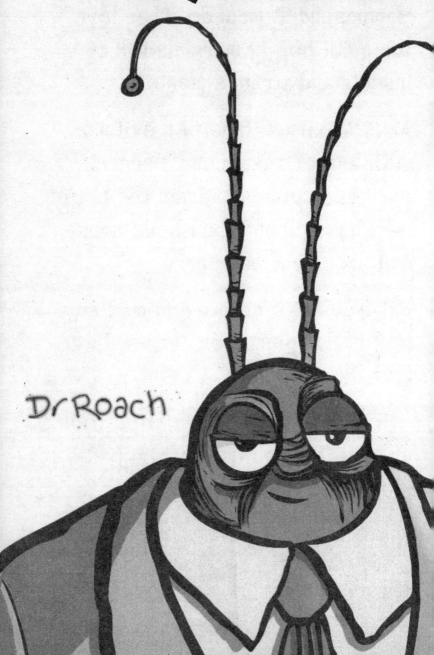